The Magic School Bus® A Science CHAPTER BOOK

SPACE EXPLORERS

SCHOLASTIC INC.
New York   Toronto   London   Auckland   Sydney
Mexico City   New Delhi   Hong Kong   Buenos Aires

Written by Eva Moore.

Illustrations by Ted Enik.

Based on *The Magic School Bus* books
written by Joanna Cole and illustrated by Bruce Degen.

The author would like to thank Dr. Tom Jones
for his expert advice in preparing
this manuscript.

ISBN 0-439-11493-4

24

4 5 6 7 8/0

Designed by Peter Koblish

Printed in the U.S.A.

40

INTRODUCTION

Hi, my name is Carlos. I am one of the kids in Ms. Frizzle's class.

Maybe you've heard of Ms. Frizzle. (Sometimes we just call her the Friz.) She is a terrific teacher — but a little strange. One of her favorite subjects is science, and she knows *everything* about it.

She takes us on lots of field trips in the Magic School Bus. Believe me, it's not called *magic* for nothing! We never know what's going to happen when we get on that bus.

Ms. Frizzle likes to surprise us, but we can usually tell when she is planning a special lesson — we just look at what she's wearing.

A few months ago, Ms. Frizzle showed up in an astronaut jumpsuit. We had just started a unit on the solar system, so we thought Ms. Frizzle was dressed up to get us in the mood. Of course, we couldn't actually take a field trip to outer space. (Ha-ha.) But the joke was on us. Let me tell you what happened. . . .

CHAPTER 1

I stuffed my homework in my backpack and ran out the door. I was in a hurry to get to school. Today was Solar System Day. Our homework was to write a report on one of the nine planets. My report was on Mars, my favorite. I just knew my report would be the best!

But that wasn't the only reason I was in a hurry. I had finally finished putting together Rocco the Rockhound Robot — a remote control rover I made from a kit. I'd been working on him for weeks — there must have been a zillion parts. Now Rocco was ready to roll, and I was taking him to school for show-and-tell.

When I got to class, Ms. Frizzle was hanging up a chart of the solar system.

Our Solar System

The solar system is the sun and all the bodies that orbit around it — the nine planets, their moons, asteroids (chunks of rock), and comets (balls of ice and dust).

Sun

The sun is the center of our solar system.

The sun supplies ALL the light and ALMOST ALL the heat for EVERYTHING else in the solar system. No planet, moon, comet, or asteroid has any light of its own.

OUR SOLAR *SYSTEM

* The word SOLAR comes from the Latin word SOL, which means SUN.

PLUTO
NEPTUNE
URANUS
SATURN
JUPITER
MARS
VENUS
MERCURY
ASTEROID BELT
SUN
THE MOON
EARTH

One by one the rest of the class came in. They crowded around to look at Rocco. "Cool toy, Carlos!" said Dorothy Ann. (Most of the time we call her D.A.)

Rocco was modeled after *Sojourner,* the first robot rover to explore Mars. But Rocco looked more like a dog than a robot. As he rolled along on his wheels, his head turned from side to side and his tail wagged. He even made a little beeping noise as he moved. It sounded something like *yip, yip, yip.*

But the best thing about Rocco was his rock pocket — a secret compartment in his back. When I pushed a button on the remote, the rock pocket opened and out popped a built-in mechanical arm with a scoop at the end.

The scoop could be dragged along the ground to pick up rocks and soil. Another button on the remote turned the arm and dumped the stuff into the rock pocket. It was the neatest way to find rocks for my collection.

"Rocco isn't a toy," I said. "He's a robot rock collector." I pushed the button to open

Rocco's rock pocket. Inside were some rocks and reddish clay soil that Rocco had scooped up on the way to school.

"This soil looks a lot like the soil on Mars," I said.

Ralphie laughed. "No way," he said. "Mars's soil is green, just like Martians."

"You've got rocks in your head, Ralphie," I said. "That stuff about little green men on Mars is pure science fiction. Mars is actually called the red planet because of the rust in its soil."

"Well, I heard that there may have been life on Mars long ago," Phoebe said. "Maybe they had little green men then."

"You guys don't know anything," Keesha said. "Nothing could live on Mars — it's too cold."

Ms. Frizzle put an end to the argument. "I think the best way to settle this is with our own eyes. Everyone, to the bus! Mars is only forty-nine million miles away. We can be there before lunch."

I tucked Rocco under my arm and followed the Friz to the parking lot. The bus looked a little different than usual. For one thing, there were a couple of huge rockets sticking out the back.

"If I'd known we were going to outer space today I would have brought a bigger lunch," Arnold said as we climbed aboard.

"Buckle your seat belts," the Friz called. "A regular spaceship would take at least nine months to get to Mars. But this is the Magic School Bus. We'll be there in a jiffy!" She fired the rockets and we blasted off.

All Planets Travel Around the Sun
by Arnold

Each planet travels around the sun — or revolves — in its own path, or orbit. The farther the planet is from the sun, the longer it takes to revolve.

Earth is the third planet from the sun. It takes 365 days (one year) to make one revolution.

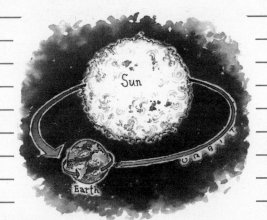

Spring + summer + fall + winter = 1 year

All Planets Spin

by Phoebe

The planets spin like tops as they revolve around the sun. Some planets spin very fast; some spin very slowly.

Earth spins around, or rotates, once every 24 hours. This is what makes day and night.

1 rotation = one daytime and one nighttime

CHAPTER 2

The great power of the rockets gave the bus enough speed to break away from Earth's gravity. We zoomed through the atmosphere into dark, airless space.

Earth's Protector
by Keesha

The atmosphere is the thin layer of air that surrounds and protects Earth. The atmosphere is held down by Earth's gravity. Without gravity, the air we breathe would fly off into space.

A Word from Dorothy Ann

Gravity is the force within a star or planet that pulls objects toward its center.

Once we were going fast enough, the Friz turned off the rockets. Right away, strange things started to happen. I had been holding Rocco on my lap. But I let go of him for a second — and he floated up to the ceiling!

At the same time, Ralphie yelled, "Hey, I can fly!" He had unbuckled his seat belt and was floating above us like Peter Pan.

"That's because we're weightless while we stay in orbit around Earth," Ms. Frizzle explained. "With the engines off, we're no longer being pulled toward the floor of the bus by gravity, so our bodies can float around."

"I've got to try it!" Keesha said. She unbuckled her seat belt and moved too quickly, spinning around in a somersault.

Soon we were all bumping into one another as we tumbled around inside the space-bus. We had to hold on to seat backs to steady ourselves.

Arnold was floating upside down near a window. "Look at Earth!" he said. "It's so beautiful from up here."

We all floated over to see. Earth was a blue-and-brownish-green sphere surrounded by swirling white clouds. Home sweet home.

Earth: "The Perfect Planet"
by Arnold

Earth is the perfect distance from the sun for life — it's not too hot and not too cold. It has water and gases, such as oxygen, that living things need.

It also has an atmosphere to protect it from harmful rays from the sun.

> All of this makes Earth a perfect place for animals and plants to live and grow.

Earth

"Earth is one of the four rocky planets, along with Mercury, Venus, and Mars," the Friz said. "But as you can see, most of the surface is covered with water. Some people think a better name for our planet would be Ocean."

There was a lot of water covering Earth. I couldn't believe how small the planet looked from space.

"Hey — there's the moon!" Wanda called. "Or at least half of it."

"The whole moon is there, Wanda," said Ms. Frizzle. "But we only see the part that is lit up by the sun's light."

13

The Orb that Orbits

by Wanda

The moon orbits Earth, just as Earth orbits the sun. One orbit takes 29 ½ days.

The moon seems to change shape because we see different amounts of its sunlit side as it travels around Earth.

I remembered that the moon is covered with rocks. "Ms. Frizzle," I said, "could we stop here? I always wanted some moon rocks for my collection."

"Sure thing, Carlos!" Ms. Frizzle fired some engines to change our direction. We slowed down as we came near the bright side of the moon. It was covered with deep pits and craters that looked like huge bowls. We landed in one of the wide craters with a thud.

"Put on your space helmets, everyone!" Ms. Frizzle instructed us, showing us how to strap on our breathing equipment. "You won't be able to breathe without the oxygen tanks. There's not a breath of air out there."

Since sound can't travel without air, we all had radios in our helmets so we could talk with one another.

I stepped carefully off the bus onto the dusty ground. Wow, I could hardly believe it. "I feel like Neil Armstrong," I said. "One small step for Carlos . . ."

Moon Walk
by Carlos

On July 20, 1969, American astronaut Neil Armstrong became the first person to set foot on the moon. He was one of three men in the Apollo 11 crew.

Millions and millions of people around the world watched on TV. Armstrong said, "That's one small step for man, one giant leap for mankind."

Between 1969 and 1972, twelve U.S. astronauts walked on the moon. They brought back 855 pounds of rocks and soil for scientists to study.

"Watch your step," the Friz told us. "The moon has gravity, but it's much weaker than on Earth. You're going to be much lighter on your feet here than you are at home."

From the Desk of Ms. Frizzle

Ms. Frizzle's Guide to Gravity

The pull of gravity depends on the mass of the planet, moon, or other body in space. Usually, the larger the body, the more mass it has. The moon is much smaller than Earth, so it has much less gravity.

If you weigh 75 pounds on Earth, you would weigh only 12½ pounds on the moon.

"Wheee!" called Ralphie. "This is better than a trampoline." He jumped easily off the ground, came back down, then bounced up.

Soon we were all leaping and laughing. D.A. and Keesha started a game of leapfrog.

"I can leap like a real frog!" Keesha said.

"I can jump like a cat!" D.A. said. "Come to think of it, I now weigh about the same as my cat does on Earth."

We were having so much fun, I almost forgot the reason we had come here in the first place.

"Rocks!" I said. "It's time to put Rocco to work."

I bent over and set Rocco down — but I didn't see Tim jumping behind me. He came down and knocked me over. And Rocco flew out of my hands! As I fell, I landed on Rocco's remote control and accidentally hit the *on* button. Oh, no! Rocco's rockets fired up and he blasted off into space!

"Rocco!" I cried. I reached up to grab him, but he zoomed away. I could see his tail wagging as he went. Poor Rocco! He shot off into the darkness. He could be lost in space forever. What would I do without him?

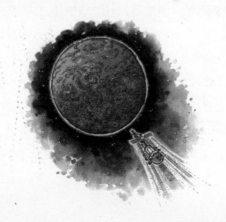

CHAPTER 3

"Hurry!" I yelled. "We've got to rescue Rocco."

Rocco was speeding farther and farther into space. If we didn't get going fast, we'd never be able to catch up with him.

As soon as everyone was aboard the space-bus, Ms. Frizzle fired the rockets and we took off after my little robot. Once we were out of orbit we were no longer weightless. We could walk around on the bus again.

"I'm sorry I bumped into you on the moon, Carlos," Tim said. "I hope we can get Rocco back."

"It's okay," I said. "It was an accident."

"Keep an eye out, kids. We might see an asteroid or two," Ms. Frizzle said. "They're chunks of rock."

From D.A.'s Notebook
Space Rocks

Asteroids can be tiny or hundreds of miles wide. Ceres, the largest asteroid in our solar system, is about 600 miles across.

Ceres
(the largest asteroid)

Earth

Most asteroids stay in orbit between Mars and Jupiter in what we call the asteroid belt. Some asteroids crash together and bounce off to roam around in other parts of the solar system.

"Hey, Ms. Frizzle, what's that bright star ahead?" Phoebe asked.

"It's not a star, Phoebe," the Friz told her. "That's the planet Venus. Venus is the third brightest object we can see from Earth after the sun and the moon."

From D.A.'s Notebook
A Planet Is Not a Star

A star is a hot, glowing ball of gas that gives off heat and light.

A planet is a body that revolves around a star. It gives off no light of its own. The light we see is reflected sunlight.

D.A. had done her report on Venus. She told us that Venus is so bright because the layers of thick clouds surrounding it reflect a lot of light from the sun.

Soon we could see the swirling clouds of Venus, and it looked as if Rocco was heading straight into them!

"Rocco will be a goner if he hits those clouds," D.A. said. "They're made of sulfuric acid that would burn right through his metal skin."

Venus: "Killer Planet"
by D.A.

Venus is about the same size as Earth and is closer to us than any other planet. Venus is deadly hot all the time, and its surface is nothing but rocky plains and dead volcanoes.

No person has ever been on Venus — the carbon dioxide in its atmosphere is poisonous to earthlings. But a few space probes have landed on its hot, windy surface. (A space probe is an unmanned research craft.)

> In 1982, a Russian space probe called Venera 13 landed on Venus and sent back the first color photos of the planet's surface. The space probe lasted for only two hours before the heat destroyed its instruments and radio transmitters.
>
> Venus

Suddenly I remembered Rocco's remote control. It was in my pocket. Maybe I could use it to steer him away from those deadly clouds. I had to act fast before the planet's gravity pulled him in.

I pushed the *reverse* button. Right on! Rocco spun around and headed back toward the space-bus.

"You did it, Carlos!" Tim yelled. "Now we just have to figure out how to get him inside once he gets close enough."

But before we could even think about that, something terrible happened. A small asteroid came hurtling along. It hit Rocco and sent him spinning off again.

"Follow that robot, please!" I called to Ms. Frizzle. The space-bus zoomed off, leaving Venus in our dust.

Rocco was going so fast, soon he was just a dot in space.

"Hey, Carlos, can you use Rocco's radio signal to follow him?" Ralphie asked.

"We can try," I said. I pushed the voice button. We heard a faint sound. "*Yip, yip, yip.*"

"I've located Rocco on the radar screen," Ms. Frizzle said. She set a new course and fired the control thrusters.

We caught up with Rocco as he was approaching Mercury, the planet nearest the sun. We had to put on special goggles to block the sun's rays. We could feel the heat beating down on us. Ms. Frizzle pulled a lever that set up special heat shields around the bus.

"Mercury must be one hot planet," I said.

"The side that faces the sun is super-hot," Keesha said. She was the expert on Mercury. "But the other side is supercold. No other planet has such extremes of temperature."

Mercury: "Speedy Hotshot"
by Keesha

Mercury is like fire and ice. During the day, the temperature rises to a scorching 700°F. At night, it drops to minus 274°F.

Mercury is covered with craters like our moon. It zips around the sun very quickly but rotates very slowly. A day on Mercury is only slightly shorter than a year!

Mercury

"*Yip, yip, yip.*" Rocco's radio signal was getting fainter. On the radar screen, we could see that Rocco was about to fly past Mercury. He was headed straight for the sun!

CHAPTER 4

"*Yip, yip, yip* . . . YIP! YIP!*" Rocco's beeps sounded like a call for help.

I tried the *reverse* button on the remote again, but Rocco was out of range. All we could do was watch him on the radar screen getting nearer and nearer to the fiery sun.

"Look!" D.A. said. "Something weird is happening. Rocco has changed direction! Now he's heading for Mercury."

"Great," I said. "He'll be smashed to smithereens instead of burnt to a crisp."

"No," said Phoebe. "Rocco isn't going *down*. He's going into orbit *around* the planet!"

Sure enough, the dot on the radar screen was circling around Mercury.

"He has become a satellite," Keesha said. "He'll keep circling around Mercury just like the moon orbits Earth."

"That's lucky for us," Ms. Frizzle said. "Now we have a chance to rescue him."

"How?" Ralphie asked. "We can't just fly up and grab him."

Ms. Frizzle got that twinkle in her eye. "Well, Ralphie, you'll be surprised to know that's just what Carlos and I plan to do!"

"Huh?" I said.

"You bet! You've seen pictures of astronauts repairing satellites out in space, right?" Ms. Frizzle asked. "Just like them, we'll be wearing tether wires. We'll be attached to the Magic Space Bus so we can't float off."

"But we'll burn up in the sun's heat!" I protested.

"Not so, Carlos," the Friz replied. She reached into a compartment and pulled out two shiny gold-coated umbrellas. "I happen to have here the very latest in parasol technology.

These parasols are made of special material that reflects heat and light. They'll protect us from the sun's rays."

First we had to get closer to Rocco. Ms. Frizzle pushed a button on the instrument panel, and we zoomed off toward Mercury.

From the Desk of Ms. Frizzle

How to Fly a Spaceship

The secret to space travel is control thrusters! They're small rockets in the front and back of the spacecraft used to steer the spacecraft. They are mounted so that they can fire in all directions — up and down, left and right. When you fire a rocket on the left, the spaceship will turn right.

Rudder and speed brake

Forward control thrusters

Rear control thrusters

The Magic Space Bus was now right between the sun and the planet. The sun looked twice as large as it does from Earth. Our goggles protected our eyes from its strong light.

Sunlight, Sun Bright
by Carlos

Our sun is an enormous glowing ball of very hot hydrogen gas. All around the fireball, a superhot gas halo called the corona fans out millions of miles into space.

The sun is so huge that one million Earths could fit inside it.

Ms. Frizzle and I got into our space suits and entered the airlock, a small room with a hatch overhead.

When the airlock was closed, we put on our helmets and turned on the oxygen. Next we let out all the air in the room. Then Ms. Frizzle checked our tether wires.

"All set! Open the hatch, Carlos. We're ready to go."

What if my tether broke? I'd be floating in space forever. But I had to save Rocco.

I floated out behind Ms. Frizzle. The light was almost blinding. We opened our parasols and quickly strapped them to our backs. Now we could see better and move around above the bus.

I caught sight of a dark object floating near my head — Rocco! I reached up . . . but it was no good. He was too far away.

"Let out more of your tether, Carlos," the Friz said over the radio. "You've nearly got him."

I didn't want to get too far from the bus. I let out the line, but the movement started me tumbling around. I went over and over in a wild somersault. Space swirled around me.

"Whoa, there!" Ms. Frizzle said. She caught hold of my feet and stopped the spinning.

"Whew!" I said. "Thanks, Ms. Frizzle. I was getting dizzy."

Now Rocco was just a few feet away. With Ms. Frizzle still holding on to my feet, I stretched forward. My fingers wrapped around Rocco's tail, and I pulled him to me. "Got him!"

Everyone on the bus cheered when they saw Rocco was back safely — especially Tim.

"Now, class," Ms. Frizzle said, "it's time to beat the heat and get out of here. This sun is hot stuff!"

From the Desk of Ms. Frizzle

How Hot Is the Sun?

The surface of the sun is almost 10,000°F. But the inner core is much, much hotter — 27 *million*°F. Just one spark that hot could set fire to everything within 60 miles!

Even with all that power, our sun is just an average star. Some stars are even bigger and hotter!

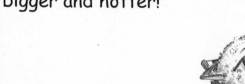

CHAPTER 5

On our way back to Mars, we whizzed past Venus and the moon. I wished I had gotten some moon rocks, but I was glad to have Rocco back. Maybe we'd have better luck collecting rocks on Mars.

As we zoomed past Earth, Ms. Frizzle had to steer around something that looked like a giant shiny insect in space. I knew it really wasn't an insect. It was a space station in orbit around Earth!

"Sun power at work!" the Friz exclaimed. "Those huge solar panels use energy from the sun's rays to keep the space station supplied with power. Scientists can live and work in the station for months at a time."

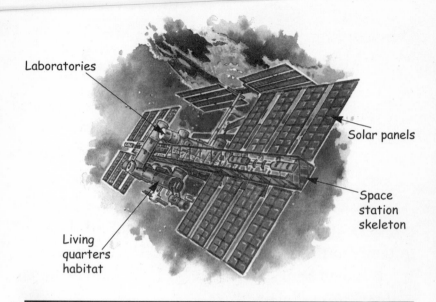

Laboratories

Solar panels

Space station skeleton

Living quarters habitat

Sun Power

by Phoebe

In empty space, there is no air — and no weather! That means no cloudy days, so a lot of sunshine is available to make solar electricity.

"Cool!" D.A. said. "I'd like to work in a space station someday."

"Not me," said Arnold. "It would be too weird floating around weightless day after day."

"You'd get used to it, Arnold," D.A said. "Besides, there's plenty of exercise equipment to help you stay in shape."

"Another reason not to go," Arnold muttered. Gym was not his favorite class.

We were all glued to the window as the bus circled the space station, then flew off again toward Mars.

Suddenly Arnold yelled, "Ms. Frizzle, there's something following us!" He was pointing to a bright streak of light that seemed to be moving very fast in our direction.

"It's a comet!" cried Arnold. "I just read a book about how a comet smashed into Jupiter a few years ago. This one looks like it's going to smash into us!"

"According to my research," D.A. said, reading from her laptop, "comets orbit the sun just like planets."

From D.A.'s Notebook
It's a Bird!
It's a Plane! It's a Comet!

Comets are balls of dust, ice, and rock. When warmed by the sun, the comet's ice changes into gas and forms a tail that carries the rock and dust along. A comet's tail can be millions of miles long.

Comets sometimes pass near Earth on their orbits around the sun. They look like long-tailed, fuzzy stars. But they don't have light of their own. The sun's reflected light gives them their flashy good looks.

The comet was gaining on us.

"Hold on!" Ms. Frizzle said. "We're going to need some extra rocket power to keep ahead of the comet. Three . . . two . . . one . . . firing rockets!"

With a whoosh, the space-bus shot forward. But the comet was right behind. It seemed to be getting closer. And now we had another problem. Suddenly we were surrounded by huge boulders floating through space.

"Asteroids," Ms. Frizzle said. "Big ones. Hold on, everyone! Looks like we're in for a bumpy ride."

Boulders came rushing at us as the Friz wildly punched buttons on the instrument panel. The bus zigged right, then zagged left, narrowly missing a huge asteroid. "Aha!" Ms. Frizzle cried. "Gotcha!" She didn't look scared. In fact, you would think that she was actually having *fun*!

"Look out, Ms. Frizzle!" Ralphie called. "There's another giant rock ahead!"

"Don't worry, Ralphie," Ms. Frizzle said.

"I'm getting the hang of this now." The bus dodged the giant asteroid and slipped between two smaller ones.

"We'll never get away from the comet at this speed!" Arnold complained. "Are any of these asteroids large enough for us to land on, Ms. Frizzle?"

"Good thinking, Arnold," the Friz said. "Here's one that should do."

Ms. Frizzle set the space-bus down on the bumpy surface of the large asteroid. We made it just in time. A second later the comet sped by above us. It grew smaller and smaller, until it disappeared in the dark beyond.

"That was awesome!" Tim said when the comet was gone.

"That was *scary*!" Arnold said.

"Where are we, Ms. Frizzle?" I asked. "How much farther to Mars?"

Ms. Frizzle pulled out her map of the solar system. "We were so busy getting away from the comet, we skipped right past it, I'm afraid," she said. "We're now in the asteroid belt, between Mars and Jupiter. We'll have to backtrack a few million miles. No problem."

Ms. Frizzle fired the rockets to turn the bus back toward Mars, but there was a strange grinding sound.

Uh-oh.

CHAPTER 6

"Uh-oh," Ms. Frizzle said. "The rocket controls are not responding. I can't shut the rockets off or turn the bus around."

"I'm not surprised," Keesha said. "Nothing is going right on this trip."

The space-bus left the asteroid belt and headed farther into space.

Ms. Frizzle tried to cheer us up. "I'm sure we'll be able to figure out how to fix the rockets. In the meantime, we're on a course for Jupiter, the biggest planet in our solar system. I've always wanted to visit the outer planets."

From the Desk of Ms. Frizzle

Out of Sight!

The outer planets are the planets in our solar system that are farthest from the sun — Jupiter, Saturn, Uranus, Neptune, and Pluto.

According to the distance gauge on the instrument panel, we were more than three hundred million miles from Earth.

"That means we're more than *four hundred* million miles from the sun," Ms. Frizzle said. "There's not much heat or light this far out. The rocket controls could be frozen. I'll have to go into the engine room and check them out." She grabbed a flashlight and headed for the tunnel at the back of the bus that led to the engine room.

We all looked at one another. "What's

going to happen if Ms. Frizzle can't fix the rockets?" Keesha asked.

"I don't want to think about it," said Ralphie.

Arnold pointed his finger at me. "This is all your fault, Carlos," he said. "We're in this mess because of that robot thing you brought along."

"Go easy on Carlos," Tim said. "It was my fault that Rocco blasted off the moon."

"Stop arguing!" Phoebe begged. "I'm sure Ms. Frizzle will take care of everything."

"Hey, look!" D.A. called. "There's Jupiter! I can see the Great Red Spot."

We forgot about the rocket trouble as we crowded around the windows to see Jupiter. It was an amazing sight, with gray, brown, blue, and orange stripes all around it.

"Those stripes are really clouds of gas. The gas is always swirling around because the planet spins so fast," Tim explained. He had done his report on Jupiter. "Jupiter makes one full rotation every ten hours — more than twice as fast as Earth so its days are really short. And Jupiter is windy, too. The Great Red Spot is actually a huge, raging storm. It's as big as three Earths side by side.

"Everything about Jupiter is super-sized," he went on. "It weighs as much as 318 Earths! It has sixteen moons — four of them are larger than planets. But they're moons because they orbit Jupiter, not the sun."

Jupiter: "The Gas Giant"
by Tim

More than 1,300 Earths could fit inside Jupiter. It has tremendous gravity. If you stood on Jupiter, you would weigh $2\frac{1}{2}$ times more than on Earth.

But you couldn't stand on Jupiter any more than you could stand on a cloud — the surface is all gas (mostly hydrogen). And it's deadly cold, more than minus 227°F. You could even get struck by lightning from Jupiter's clouds.

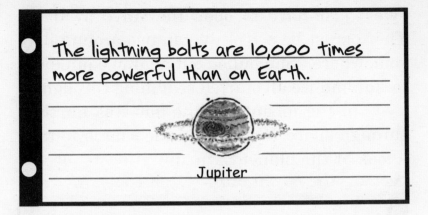

The lightning bolts are 10,000 times more powerful than on Earth.

Jupiter

"Well, we're all going to be in supersized trouble if Ms. Frizzle doesn't get the rockets fixed fast," Arnold said. "We're passing Jupiter and going even farther into space."

Just then Ms. Frizzle came out of the tunnel. She gave us the bad news. "The heating coils that warm the rocket controls are out," she reported. "It looks like one of the main heat valves is frozen shut."

Keesha shook her head. "We're in for it now," she said. "If we can't turn around, the space-bus will keep on going, out past Uranus and Neptune and Pluto . . . out of the solar system. Oh dear, oh dear . . . oh dear . . ."

"Not to worry, Keesha," Ms. Frizzle said.

"We'll just have to open the valve by hand. There must be a tool we can use around here somewhere." She pulled out a large equipment locker and we all started searching through it.

In the meantime, the bus was hurtling through space. We stopped the search to take a look at the planet Saturn.

Saturn: "Queen of the Planets"
by Phoebe

Saturn is like a queen with rings and moon jewels — more rings and moons than any other planet. The rings are made of bits and chunks of rock and ice — some as tiny as grains of sand and some as big as a house.

Saturn

> Saturn is a fast-spinning gas giant. It is mostly hydrogen and helium. It spins so fast that it bulges at its equator, making it flatter at the poles than any other planet.

"Saturn is really big," Arnold said.

"It's the second-largest planet," Phoebe told him. She was excited. This was *her* planet.

"Next to Earth, I think Saturn is the most beautiful planet in the solar system," she said. "Look at those rings that go around the planet — there are thousands of them."

We watched as Saturn and its biggest moon, called Titan, grew farther and farther away. Even Tim was getting worried now. (Even *I* was getting worried now.) In space, there is no air to cause friction to stop a moving object. If we didn't get the rockets working, we'd fly out of our solar system into deep space. We'd keep going forever and ever. We'd be lost in space!

CHAPTER 7

"Hooray!" Ms. Frizzle yelled. She pulled a wrench out of the equipment box. "I'll have that fuel valve opened before you can say 'Frizolar system'!"

While Ms. Frizzle was in the engine room, we came upon another planet surrounded by rings. It was a beautiful blue-green color, but there was something really weird about it.

"Hey, that's my planet — Uranus!" Wanda exclaimed. "See how it looks like it's on its side?" she said. "All the other planets are tilted slightly as they orbit the sun, but Uranus leans way over. It sure looks topsy-turvy."

"You'd be topsy-turvy, too, if you were stuck this far out in space," I told Wanda. "We're more than one and a half *billion* miles from home!"

Uranus: "Strangest Planet"
by Wanda

Uranus stands out because of its strange tilt. Its poles point almost directly toward the sun. Scientists think some moon or asteroid smacked into the planet billions of years ago and made it tilt like that. It's a gas giant like Jupiter and Saturn, and its pretty blue-green color comes from methane gas in its atmosphere.

Uranus

The bus seemed to be going faster and faster. We zipped past Uranus and onward toward Neptune. Where *was* Ms. Frizzle?

Even though we had the jitters, we couldn't help oohing and aahing as we passed the icy blue Neptune.

"Hey," Ralphie said, "it's my planet. It looks just like a marble."

Neptune: "Stormy Blue Marble"
by Ralphie

Neptune is very far away from the sun and very cold. We didn't know much about it until recently, because Neptune can't be seen without a telescope. (Neither can Pluto.)

In 1989 the spacecraft Voyager 2 sent back the first close-up photos. Voyager 2 showed that this gas

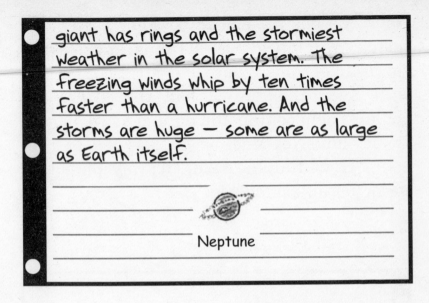

giant has rings and the stormiest
weather in the solar system. The
freezing winds whip by ten times
faster than a hurricane. And the
storms are huge — some are as large
as Earth itself.

Neptune

Then we were all surprised to find out
that Pluto, the smallest planet in the solar
system, isn't always the farthest planet from
the sun.

"Sometimes Pluto's orbit brings it closer
to the sun than Neptune is," Ralphie told us.
He had done his report on both planets. "But
now Pluto is back in its usual place."

Pluto and Charon: "Planetary Pair"
by Ralphie

Pluto is smaller than our moon — and so far away that the sun is just a very bright star in Pluto's black sky. It's also the coldest planet, with an average surface temperature of minus 369°F.

No space probes have gone out toward Pluto yet, so we don't know very much about it. We do know that its moon, Charon, is an unusual sidekick. Charon is more than half the size of Pluto! They revolve around each other so closely that they are called a double-planet system.

Pluto

Charon

At last Ms. Frizzle came out of the engine room. "It looks like I'm going to need some help with that valve," she said. "Carlos, come along with me. You're good at fixing things."

I started to follow Ms. Frizzle into the tunnel. Then I heard something behind me. "*Yip, yip, yip.*" Rocco was right on my heels.

"I think he wants to come, too," I said. I picked him up and crawled into the tunnel after the Friz.

Once we were in the engine room, Ms. Frizzle turned to me with a frown. "I didn't want to say anything in front of the others," she said, "but we have a problem. I can see the stuck valve all right, but I can't reach it. My hand is too big to fit through the opening around the valve. I thought your hand might fit."

She leaned over and pointed her flashlight at the opening. It was close to the floor and very small. There was no way I could get my hand inside.

Suddenly Rocco started rolling around in a circle. "*Yip, yip, yip,*" he barked. His tail wagged back and forth.

"You know something, Ms. Frizzle," I said. "Rocco's mechanical arm would fit in there easily. I used the remote to close his built-in arm around the valve. Rocco's motor might be strong enough to twist the valve open."

"Give it a try!" said the Friz. "This playful pup of yours might turn out to be a hero after all."

We held our breath as I pushed the button to activate Rocco's arm. We heard a whirring noise, then a clank as the scoop clamped around the valve. The motor slowed down for a moment — then purred back to life. "Did it work?" I asked.

Ms. Frizzle put her hand up to the heating coils. "They're getting warm, all right!" Ms. Frizzle beamed. "Three cheers for Rocco and Carlos."

A short while later, all the rockets were

back on line. The bus made a wide arc and turned around Pluto and Charon.

"Mars or bust!" the Friz exclaimed. She fired the main rockets, and we were out of there!!

CHAPTER 8

We made it safely through the asteroid belt and headed for Mars.

As we sped along, we flew through bands of tiny particles. "Meteoroids," Ms. Frizzle explained, "space dust left behind when comets pass. Every day one thousand pounds of the stuff falls to Earth."

"No wonder my room is always dusty," Arnold said.

Soon we could see a warm reddish sphere in front of us.

"Well, what do you know?" Ralphie said. "Mars really is red." He sounded disappointed that it wasn't green.

When we got closer, we could see hazy white clouds wrapped around the planet.

"Mars may be red," Ms. Frizzle said, "but it's not red-hot. Those clouds are frozen carbon dioxide and ice. You'll be glad to have your insulated space suits on when we go out exploring."

Mars Weather Report:
Freezing and windy

by Carlos

Bundle up — the average temperature on Mars is minus 80°F. Some parts of Mars can get pretty warm during the day — up to 70°F. But at night they get supercold — down to minus 207°F.

Mars also has fierce windstorms and huge tornadoes called dust devils. They have less power than tornadoes, but they can produce columns of dust 5 miles high.

The space-bus landed in a wide valley. There were tall red cliffs all around. The sky looked orange.

"Mars is only half the size of Earth," I pointed out as we put on our space suits, "but some of its volcanoes and canyons can make ours look puny."

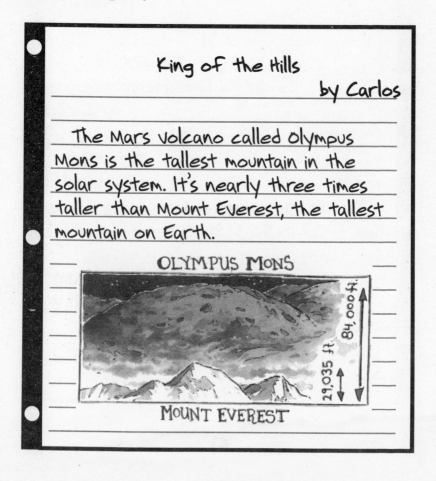

King of the Hills

by Carlos

The Mars volcano called Olympus Mons is the tallest mountain in the solar system. It's nearly three times taller than Mount Everest, the tallest mountain on Earth.

OLYMPUS MONS

29,035 ft.   84,000 ft.

MOUNT EVEREST

The dusty orange-red ground outside the space-bus looked like a desert covered with rocks of all sizes. I could hardly wait to turn Rocco loose out there.

We climbed off the bus. I felt fifty pounds lighter than usual. That's because Martian gravity is only a third as strong as Earth's. A person who weighs seventy-five pounds on Earth is only twenty-five pounds on Mars.

"Wow!" I said. "There are some fantastic rocks around here." In fact, the ground was covered with rocks. Most of them were too big for Rocco to handle. Then I spotted an area filled with smaller pieces of rock.

Perfect! I thought. I pointed Rocco in that direction. "Go get 'em!" I said, and pushed the remote.

I couldn't believe my eyes. Rocco took off like lightning — much faster than he'd ever gone before.

What's with this remote? I wondered. I pushed the *stop* button, but Rocco kept on going. He zipped right past the small rocks and headed out toward a boulder in the distance.

"Help!" I called. "This remote has gone wacky! Rocco is running away!" The other kids heard me on their helmet radios. "He went that way," I said. We all took off after the runaway robot, making great leaping strides.

"Hurry!" I yelled. "We'll lose him!"

When we got to the boulder, we could see the tracks of Rocco's wheels leading to the edge of a small crater.

I started to run toward the crater when Tim yelled, "Hold it, Carlos. We've got to get out of here. . . . Look!"

We turned to see what he was pointing at: a huge column of dust whirling up from the ground.

"It's a dust devil," I yelled, "a Martian tornado!"

At the word *tornado*, everyone turned and took off for the space-bus.

I knew that the dust devil was dangerous — the high winds stirred up tons of dust. When I did my report, I had read that dust devils were slow-moving storms. I hoped it was true. I *had* to find Rocco.

I slid down the side of the crater and followed Rocco's tracks. The sky seemed to be turning pink. I looked up and saw the top of the dust devil. It was coming my way!

"Rocco, where are you?" I called. The tracks led to a pile of rocks. I stopped in amazement. There was Rocco, dragging his scoop along the rocky ground. In one quick movement, he emptied a scooper full of red chunks into his rock pocket. With a wag of his tail, the mechanical arm folded up and the rock pocket closed.

There was no time to spare. I grabbed my rockhound, tucked him under my arm, and climbed out of the crater as fast as I could go. The dust devil was right behind me as I raced to the waiting bus!

Ms. Frizzle opened the door. "Good to see you — and Rocco," she said. "I was just about to send out a search party. When that dust devil hits, we won't be able to see a thing."

I buckled myself into my seat and held Rocco in my lap. Everyone else was already buckled up.

In a second, the space-bus lifted off. We rose higher and higher above the red planet. We could see the dust storm spreading out above the planet's surface.

"I hope we can come back someday," I said. "I have a feeling there is a lot more to learn about Mars."

Mars: "The Red and Rocky Planet"
by Carlos

Because so many space probes have been sent to study Mars, we know more about it than any other planet except Earth.

Mars is like Earth in some ways. Its day is about the same length, and it has icy polar caps. We think that at one time Mars was warmer and that floods of water carved deep channels in the surface.

In 1996 some scientists thought they had found remains of tiny life-forms in a meteorite from Mars. But they're still not sure if these are just natural patterns in the rock — or actual traces of life.

Mars

CHAPTER 9

The next day, Ms. Frizzle took us back to the solar system — but this time we didn't have to leave the classroom. She had put our reports up on the bulletin board so we could revisit the planets whenever we felt like it. Only one was missing.

"Okay, Carlos," Ms. Frizzle said. "Where's your report on Mars?"

"I think Rocco has it," I said. I pushed a button on the remote and Rocco came rolling into the room. (I had left him out in the hallway. It was part of a big surprise I had planned.)

"*Yip, yip, yip*," Rocco beeped as he came up to me. He had my report in his mouth.

The kids laughed. "Hey, Rocco, how's it going?" Ralphie said. "Seen any dust devils lately?"

I pinned my report up on the board. "Now," I said, "prepare to be amazed." I opened the rock pocket on Rocco's back. "Ta-da! Rocco the Rockhound Robot has returned with real Martian rocks!"

I took out a handful of small red chunks and passed them around for everyone to see.

"Are these really from Mars?" asked Arnold.

"They sure are!" I said. "I saw Rocco scoop them up with my own eyes."

"Unbelievable!" Tim said. "I guess he really is a rockhound at heart."

"*Yip, yip!*" Rocco said. No doubt about it.

	Distance from the Sun	Diameter*	Size Rank
Mercury	36 million miles	3,000 miles	8th largest
Venus	67 million miles	7,500 miles	6th largest
Earth	93 million miles	7,900 miles	5th largest
Mars	142 million miles	4,200 miles	7th largest
Jupiter	483 million miles	89,000 miles	Largest
Saturn	887 million miles	75,000 miles	2nd largest
Uranus	Almost 2 billion miles	31,700 miles	3rd largest
Neptune	Almost 3 billion miles	31,000 miles	4th largest
Pluto	3½ billion miles	1,400 miles	Smallest

*The diameter is the distance straight through the planet, from one pole to the other.

Our Solar System

Length of day	Length of year	Number of moons
59 Earth days	88 Earth days	0
243 Earth days	225 Earth days	0
24 hours	365 days	1
24½ Earth hours	23 Earth months	2
10 Earth hours	12 Earth years	16
10¼ Earth hours	29½ Earth years	18 for sure; probably a few more
18 Earth hours	84 Earth years	20
19 Earth hours	165 Earth years	8
6½ Earth days	249 Earth years*	1

*Pluto hasn't even made one complete orbit since it was discovered in 1930!

★ FACT & FICTION ★

It's true that space is an amazing place, but there are lots of things in this story that could never happen. Here are some of them:

1. A school bus can't really fly through space — it would not even be able to get you into orbit. Only machines that are designed for space travel can get you there. Plus, flying through space takes training. People learn about space for years before becoming astronauts.

2. Even though Carlos is a smart third-grader, he would not be able to build a robot like Rocco. Rocco was modeled after a

real rover, the *Sojourner,* and only a person trained to build robots and rockets could actually put Rocco together and make him work. It takes years of school and studying to build robots and rockets.

3. You could never see the whole solar system in one day. It's way too big! It took years for the *Voyager* space probes to explore the solar system.

4. The sun is hot stuff. Satellites that travel near the sun are equipped with special gold parasols (similar to the ones Ms. Frizzle and Carlos used) to reflect the sun's powerful rays. But people cannot fly to the sun because its heat and gravity would be too strong.

5. The asteroid belt isn't as crowded as it looks in this book and in movies. It would be easy to dodge the asteroids in the area between Mars and Jupiter. Even though there are thousands and thousands of asteroids, they are not that close together.

A Final Note from D.A.
Our Place in Space

Milky Way

   Our sun is only one of billions of stars in a galaxy called the Milky Way. A galaxy is an enormous group of stars held together by gravity. The Milky Way is only one of billions of galaxies in the universe.